Arthur Starter Book 07

ARTHUR'S
Birthday Surprise

by Marc Brown

Long tail Books

It was D.W.'s birthday. Her party was about to start.
"More balloons!" D.W. ordered.
"Yes, Your Highness," said Dad.

“More streamers!” D.W. demanded.
“More streamers, *please*,” Mom reminded her.

Ding-dong!

"My guests!" cried D.W. She ran to the front door.

"Happy birthday, D.W.!" said Emily.
The Tibble twins were right behind her.
"Where's the cake?" asked Tommy.
"Where's the ice cream?" asked Timmy.
"When do we eat?" they asked together.

“Happy Birthday dear D.W., happy birthday to you!” everyone sang.

D.W. blew out her candles. She ate her cake. She opened her presents.

But the whole time, she kept looking out the window.

“What are you waiting for?” asked Tommy.

“It’s a surprise,” D.W. said. “A surprise that’s a little late.”

Just then, the phone rang.
"Hello?" said Dad. "Oh, no . . . I see . . . Good-bye."
"What is it?" asked D.W. "What's wrong?"
"I'm afraid Mary Moo Cow can't come," Dad said.
"She's feeling sick to her stomach."
"You mean *stomachs*," said Emily. "Cows have four, you know."

“Wow, Mary Moo Cow would have been great,” said Timmy.
“I wonder if she looks as purple in person.”
“Now we’ll never know,” sighed Tommy.

“My party’s ruined!” moaned D.W.
“No, it’s not!” said Dad. “Let’s play some games.
How about Pin the Tail on the Donkey?
Won’t that be fun?”

"I know that tail's in here somewhere," muttered Dad.

“Look!” cried Emily. “It’s Mary Moo Cow!”

"I thought you couldn't come," said D.W.

"I made a moo-raculous recovery," Mary Moo Cow answered in a squeaky voice.

"What are you going to do?" D.W. asked.

"Do?" said Mary Moo Cow. "I'm going to—to entertain you, of course!"

“First comes my Udderly Amazing Magic Show.
Watch as I pull a rabbit out of a hat! Er—come out, rabbit.”

"Next, witness my incredible feats of daring.
I may be a cow, but I'm no cow-ard!"

“And last but not least, you are each entitled to one of my world-famous, wild and crazy rides. I call them—Milk Shakes!”

When it was time to leave, no one wanted to go.
"That was fun," said Emily.
"Awesome Milk Shakes," said Tommy.
"Maybe Mary Moo Cow can come
to our birthday party, too," said Timmy.

“Arthur,” said D.W. “That was the worst Mary Moo Cow imitation I’ve ever seen.”

“It was?” said Arthur.

D.W. gave him a hug.
"But it was the best present I got all day!"